MW00893660

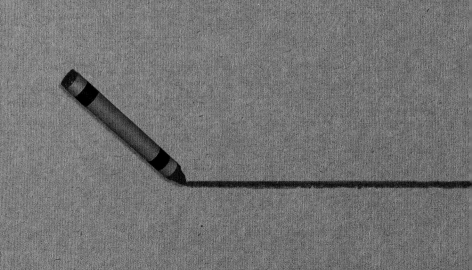

The Blue Sky Press • An Imprint of Scholastic Inc. • New York

ALL OF ME!

a book of thanks

BY MOLLY BANG

THE BLUE SKY PRESS

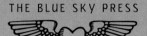

Copyright © 2009 by Molly Bang

All rights reserved. No part of this publication may be reproduced,
stored in a retrieval system, or transmitted in any form or by
any means, electronic, mechanical, photocopying, recording, or
otherwise, without written permission of the publisher.

For information regarding permission, please write to: Permissions
Department, Scholastic Inc., 557 Broadway, New York, New York 10012.

SCHOLASTIC, THE BLUE SKY PRESS, and associated logos are
trademarks and/or registered trademarks of Scholastic Inc.

Library of Congress catalog card number: 2008049692

ISBN-13: 978-0-545-04424-0 / ISBN-10: 0-545-04424-3

10 9 8 7 6 5 4 3 2 1   09 10 11 12 13

Printed in Singapore   46

First printing, September 2009

The artwork was created with crayons,
paint, and collage on paper bags.

Designed by Kathleen Westray

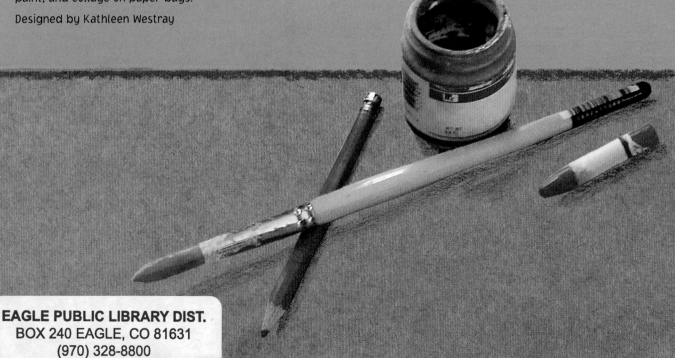

FOR

Ezra
Luca
Lily
Lucy
Luna
Maggie
Chloe
Eloise
Aliza
Teo
David
Sama
Nate
Ella
Lila
Charlie
Monika

in memory
of
General Tank

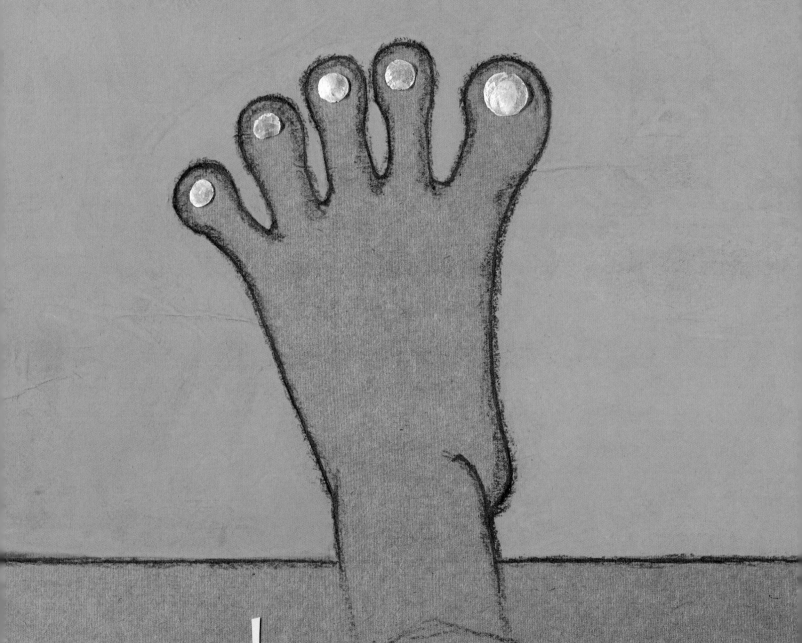

Look at my fine feet!
Thank you, feet,
for holding me up

when I stand,
and when I walk,
and when I jump!

When I sit down, I sit on my good bottom.

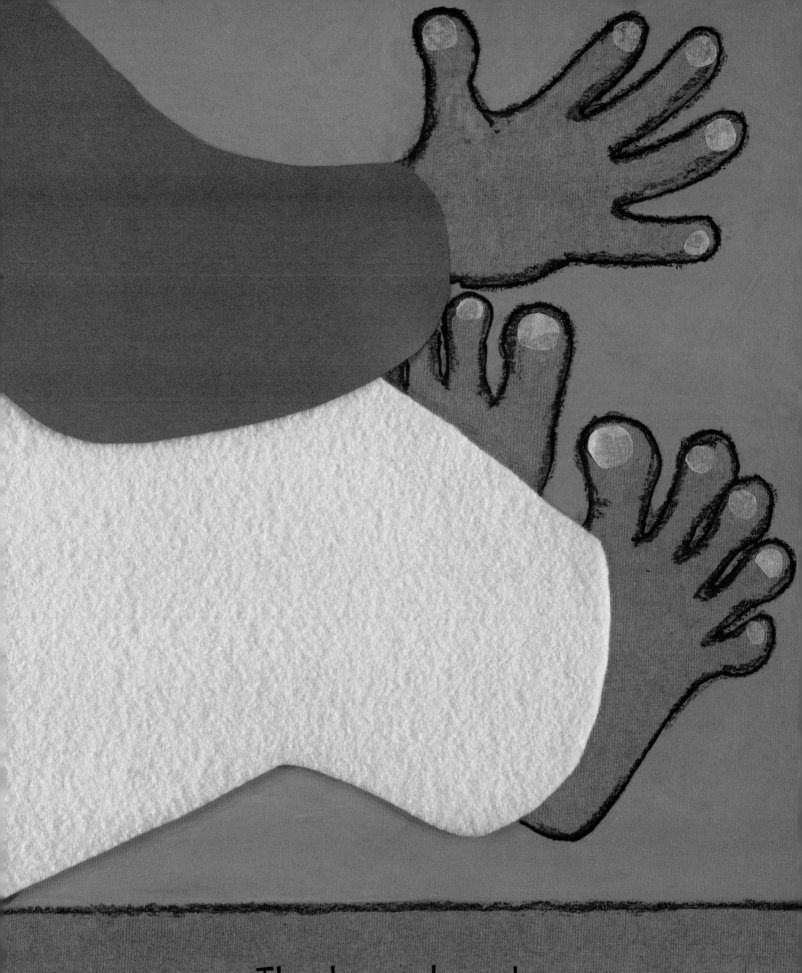

Thank goodness!

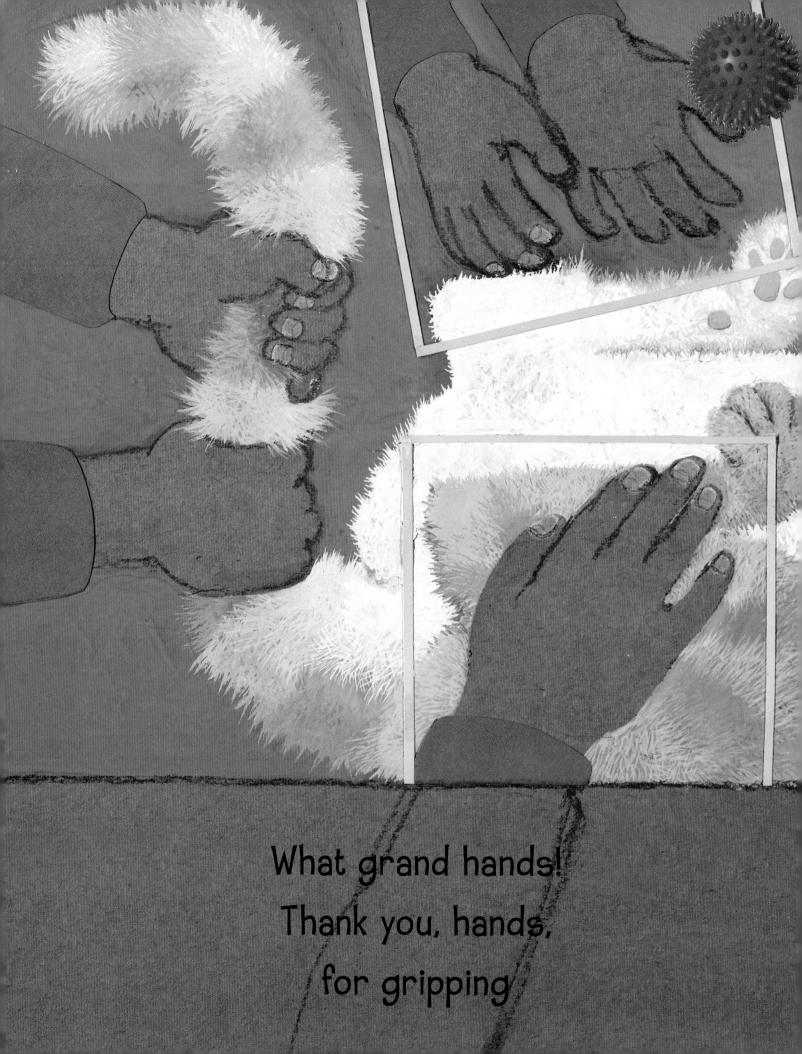

What grand hands!
Thank you, hands,
for gripping

and throwing
and patting and holding.
And for hugging.

Thank you, arms,
for hugging even more.

And look at my knees and elbows!
My knees and elbows bend whenever I ask!

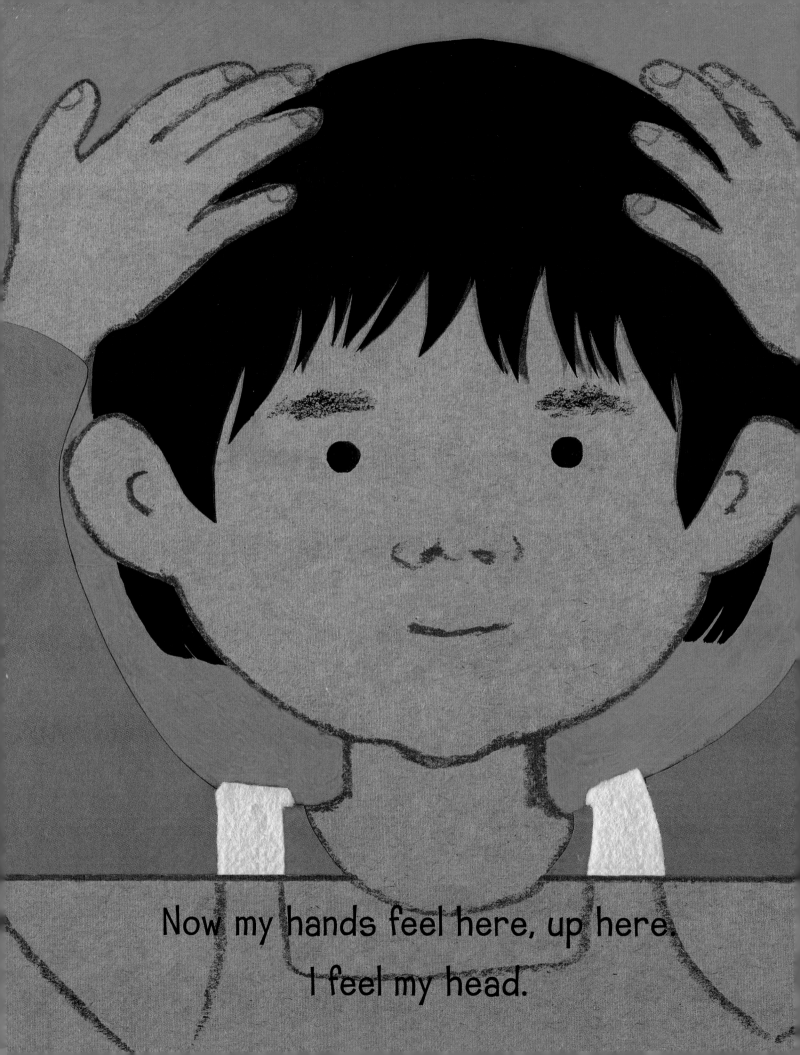

Now my hands feel here, up here.
I feel my head.

Thank you, my extraordinary head
and all your different parts.

I smile and talk and sing with my . . .
mouth.
My lips kiss Mommy and Daddy.

My teeth bite crackers. My tongue licks
ice cream. My mouth tastes all my food
before it slides down here, into my tummy.

I see with my . . .

eyes.

I see the night outside.

Inside I see light and animals, a ball,
a clock, a book, and big hands.
Whose big hands are those?

I smell with my . . . nose.
So many different smells!

(And sometimes my nose
rubs other noses.)

I listen with my . . .

ears.

Outside I hear cars rumbling.

I hear people playing music.

I hear honking, singing, barking,
and laughing. Inside I hear purring.

I hear a ticking clock.

And in between the noises, I hear . . .

SILENCE.

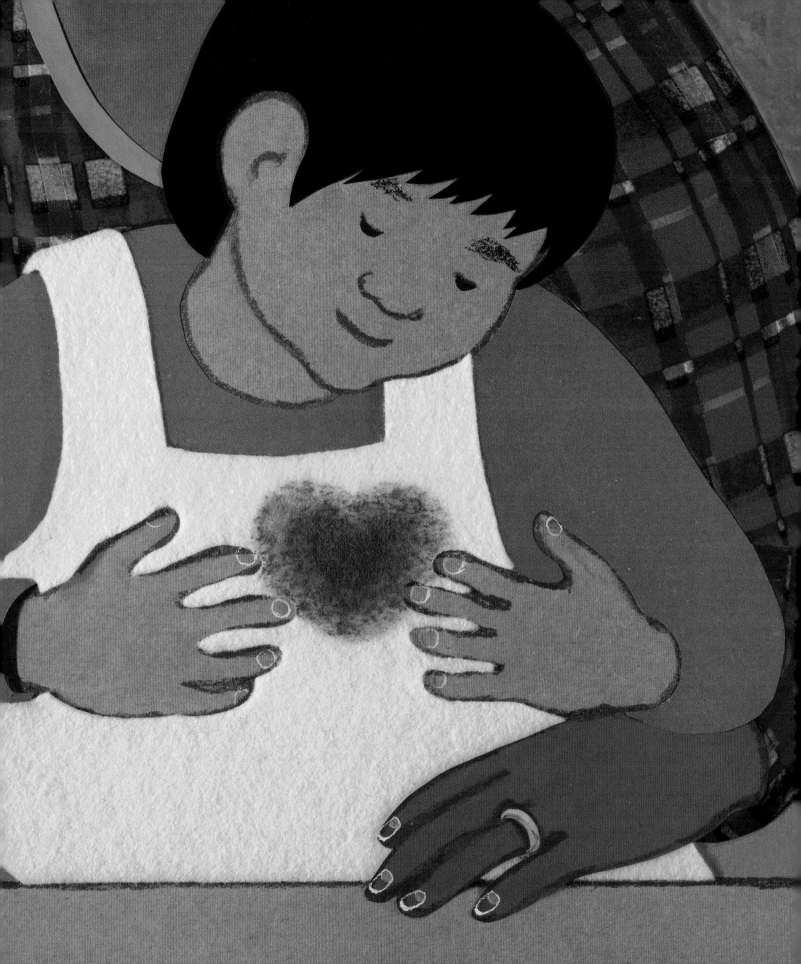

Now I feel my heart beat: thump, thump, thump.

Thank you, heart, for pumping life all through my body. Thank you, my whole body.

Today I did so many things.
Today I felt so many feelings.
I felt curious, and excited,

and angry, and brave, and sad,
and scared, and shy, and happy,
and thankful, and calm.

Today I feel loving—

loving and perfectly safe.

And right now I also know that I am part of
this whole world—this universe!

All this is my home. I am ALIVE.
And this whole universe is inside . . .

. . . all of me! What a wonder.

BOOKS ARE FUN TO MAKE!

To make this book, I needed:

PAPER BAGS. (You have to use the inside, where there is no ink printed on the paper.)

CLOTH AND PAPER. I like to cut out pieces of cloth and construction paper with scissors and glue them onto the paper-bag paper. Some-times I cut out pictures from a magazine and paste them on, too.

CRAYONS!! I made thick, strong lines with red crayon. You can color in with crayons, too. I only used red, but of course you can use ALL the colors. I think I need a new red crayon.

PAINTS. I love paint. Some of my paint is in little jars. Some paint I squeeze from tubes into scallop shells I picked up from a beach in Nova Scotia.

PAINTBRUSHES. I guess I could have painted with my fingers or with a stick. But I like brushes.

WATER. You have to rinse the paint off your brush before you use a new color. If you don't rinse your brush in clean water, all the colors mix together, and everything turns muddy gray or brown.